Out of the Question

by
Ruth Gash Taylor

Cork Hill Press
Indianapolis

CORK HILL PRESS™

Cork Hill Press
7520 East 88th Place, Suite 101
Indianapolis, Indiana 46256-1253
1-866-688-BOOK
www.corkhillpress.com

Trade Paperback Edition: 1-59408-169-7

Printed in the United States of America

1 3 5 7 9 10 8 6 4 2

OUT OF THE QUESTION

As soon as I had a chance to look over this big world — and acquired speech — I began to ask questions. One day, my poor mother cried, "Ruth, if you ask one more question, I'm going to put you in an orphans' home!"

So I asked the fatal question, "What's an orphans' home?"

I had learned — Out of the question comes an answer. I hope countless others have a thirst for knowledge, and fun testing it.

R. G. T.

WORK FROM SUN TO SUN

It is a Czech proverb that "Where the sun never comes, the doctor comes often." In the interests of your good health, every answer contains sun. You don't even need sunglasses.

1. A favorable spot

2. Novel by Ernest Hemingway

3. Australian tramp

4. England, once

5. Capricornus or winter solstice

6. Kansas

7. Alexander the Great's opinion

8. More persons pay honor to ascendant than to fallen greatness

9. Composition by Stevie Wonder

10. Helianthus

11. Florida

12. Roof, balcony or terrace

13. Instrument that indicates local apparent solar time

14. Parhelion

15. Bluegill, pumpkinseed

WORK FROM SUN TO SUN

1. A place in the sun

2. *The Sun Also Rises*

3. Sundowner

4. The empire on which the sun never sets

5. The Southern Gate of the Sun

6. The Sunflower State

7. Heaven cannot support two suns, nor earth two masters.

8. More worship the rising than the setting sun.

9. *You Are The Sunshine of My Life*

10. Sunflower

11. Sunshine State

12. Sun deck

13. Sundial

14. Sun dog

15. Sunfish

IF YOU USE YOUR HEAD...

you may save your feet, according to an old axiom. Also, by using your head, you will discover a "foot" in every answer of this exercise. Example: Infantryman — Foot soldier.

1.   Make a favorable first impression

2.   Walking

3.   Make an embarrassing blunder

4.   In the way

5.   Take a firm stand.

6.   A portion of motion picture film

7.   Highly contagious disease among cloven-hoofed animals

8.   Game directed by a quarterback

9.   Span intended to carry only pedestrians

10. Sound made by a step

11. Natural elevated areas at base of mountain range

12. Male servant

13. Flirting game

14. Comment at bottom of page, or a reference cited.

15. Movie for which Daniel Day-Lewis won Academy Award 1989

IF YOU USE YOUR HEAD

1. Put one's best foot forward

2. On foot

3. Put one's foot in one's mouth

4. Under foot

5. Put one's foot down

6. Footage

7. Foot-and-mouth disease

8. Football

9. Footbridge

10. Footfall

11. Foothills

12. Footman

13. Playing footsie

14. Footnote

15. *My Left Foot*

FAIR TOMORROW

The word "fair" often is heard in weather reports. It appears frequently, too, in our language as an adjective or part of a proper name. As the saying goes, you "bid fair" to solve all the following puzzlers, using "fair" in every answer.

1. Just and honest

2. Proverb about the certainty after trouble

3. A regional event

4. Baseball call

5. Too late for the fun; wise after the event

6. Every opportunity being given

7. Straightforwardly

8. Football call

9. A document after corrections and revisions

10. Principles and legislative program of President Harry S. Truman

11. Space outdoors for public events

12. Courtesy and moderation will help one achieve purpose.

13. A worthy object of banter

14. A euphemism for smuggling

15. Mere speech will not feed the hungry.

FAIR TOMORROW

1. Fair and square

2. "After black clouds comes the fair weather."

3. Fair

4. Fair ball

5. A day after the fair

6. A fair field and no favor

7. By fair means

8. Fair catch

9. Fair copy

10. Fair Deal

11. Fairgrounds

12. Fair and soft go far in a day.

13. Fair game

14. Fair Trade

15. Fair words butter no parsnips.

CHECKING OUT BOOK LOVERS

All answers contain the word "book". Example: Mobile lending library — Bookmobile.

1.   To compel to explain or account for

2.   According to established rules

3.   Bookkeeping term

4.   In one's opinion

5.   Keep financial records

6.   Thoroughly

7.   To accept bets as a bookmaker

8.   Something noteworthy

9.   Recorded or registered

10.   Punish severely

11.   List or register

12.   Limitations proverb

13.   Symbols of excommunication

14.   Don't contradict a person on his special subject.

15.   In disfavor

CHECKING OUT BOOK LOVERS

1. Bring to book

2. By the book

3. Close the books

4. In one's book

5. Keep books

6. Like the book

7. Make book

8. One for the books

9. On the books

10. Throw the book at

11. Book

12. "You cannot judge a book by its cover."

13. Bell, book and candle

14. Beware of a man of one book.

15. In one's black books

LET'S TAKE A DIP...

and neither diploe nor diplont shall stay you in your quest for 15 answers containing d-i-p. Example: Dangerous, infectious disease of throat — Diphtheria.

1.   Ice cream cone

2.   Practice of pensioned worker hired by same employer in another capacity

3.   Pass between China and India

4.   Reluctant move to relieve financial stress

5.   One exercising skill or tact in dealing with others

6.   Inclinometer

7.   Long-handled cup

8.   *Ursa* Major

9.   *Ursa* Minor

10. Foolish

11. Legendary serpent whose bite produces great thirst

12. Insatiable craving for alcohol

13. Rod for measuring oil in crankcase

14. Flies, gnats and mosquitoes

15. Ancient writing tablet.

LET'S TAKE A DIP

1. Double/triple dip

2. Double dipping

3. Diphu

4. Dip into savings

5. Diplomat

6. Dip needle

7. Dipper

8. Big Dipper

9. Little Dipper

10. Dippy

11. Dipsas

12. Dipsomania

13. Dipstick

14. Dipterans

15. Diptych

NOT A RED CENT

A penny saved may be a penny earned, but you can't put these cents in your piggy bank. Example: Shining brilliantly – Incandescent. Every answer contains a "cent".

1. Vocal prominence or phonetic habit of native land

2. Something inciting to action

3. Close to

4. In not too distant past

5. Celebration of 100 years

6. Part man, part horse

7. Axis

8. Force moving away from an axis

9. 100 years

10. Shaped like first quarter of the moon

11. Conformity to rules of propriety

12. Going down

13. Going up

14. Exhibiting electromagnetic radiation

15. Roman army officer

NOT A RED CENT

1. Accent

2. Incentive

3. Adjacent

4. Recent

5. Centennial

6. Centaur

7. Center

8. Centrifugal

9. Century

10. Crescent

11. Decent

12. Descent

13. Ascent

14. Fluorescent

15. Centurion

GIVE ME A BREAK!

All answers contain the word "break". Example: To commence a new project — Break ground.

1. Employ superhuman effort on the accomplishment of a small matter.

2. To partake of food

3. To start forth from a hiding place

4. Dengue

5. A wave that crests, or foams, especially against a shoreline

6. A barrier that protects a harbor or shore from full impact of waves

7. Gaining of unauthorized access

8. A major achievement or success that permits further progress

9. Headlong speed

10. First meal of the day

11. A high, wide cabinet having a central section projecting beyond end sections

12. Slang: To convulse with laughter

13. Fail to function

14. Potential difference in volts at which a normally insulating medium becomes conducting

15. Pope Adrian IV

GIVE ME A BREAK!

1. Break a butterfly on a wheel

2. Break bread

3. Break cover

4. Breakbone fever

5. Breaker

6. Breakwater

7. Breaking and entering

8. Breakthrough

9. Break-neck

10. Breakfast

11. Breakfront

12. Break up

13. Breakdown

14. Breakdown voltage

15. Nicholas Breakspear

FRUITS OF YOUR LABOR

All answers in this exercise contain the name of a fruit. Example: Tree associated with the silk industry — Mulberry.

1.   Tree that tested George Washington's honesty

2.   Symbol of hospitality

3.   When is a cuckoo allowed to cease singing?

4.   Vaudeville act that attracted barrages of vegetables

5.   One-time site of Iowa capital

6.   One of the founders of *Punch*

7.   Purplish-pink glaze used on Chinese porcelain

8.   Mobile crane

9.   Something especially desirable, or a good position

10.   Small piece of candy

11.   Quahog

12.   Novel by John Steinbeck

13.   Georgia.

14.   Divides something too small to be worth dividing

15.   Cluster of small iron balls

FRUITS OF YOUR LABOR

1. Cherry

2. Pineapple

3. After he has eaten three good meals of cherries

4. Cherry Sisters

5. Plum Grove

6. Mark Lemon

7. Peach-blow

8. Cherry-picker

9. Plum

10. Sugar plum

11. Cherry-stone clam

12. *The Grapes of Wrath*

13. Peach State

14. Take two bites of a cherry

15. Grapeshot

WORDS

The combination of sounds that make our speech. Every answer needs a word. Example: Unable to describe or talk about — Have no words for.

1.   Do utmost to put someone in the best light

2.   Proverb about feeding the hungry

3.   Quarrel

4.   Assuredly

5.   Approach someone, with a wish for conversation

6.   Disadvantage of a sharp tongue

7.   Early puzzle

8.   English poet

9.   In immediate response

10.   Exactly

11.   Act in accordance with someone's statement

12.   Three forms of gratitude

13.   Alexia

14.   Lexicon

15.   A pun

WORDS

1. Put in a good word

2. "Soft words butter no parsnips."

3. Have words with someone

4. Upon my word

5. I'd like a word with you.

6. Tart words make no friends.

7. Word square

8. William Wordsworth

9. At a word

10. In so many words

11. Take one at one's word

12. A feeling in the heart, an expression in words and a giving in return.

13. Word-blindness

14. Word book

15. Word play

PAPER CHASE

All answers contain "paper". Example: Bank notes as opposed to coins — Paper money.

1.   Documents required by international law for sailing vessels

2.   Hypothetical profits shown on a prospectus

3.   In writing or print

4.   A book

5.   Tapa

6.   Occupation

7.   Tool used for opening envelopes

8.   Argonaut

9.   Hornet

10.   A small heavy object

11.   Proverb used by Ernest Hemingway in *For Whom the Bell Tolls*

12.   Proverb about impressionability

13.   Novel aspect of the Alger Hiss spy case

14.   One-time beauty aid

15.   Insect trap

PAPER CHASE

1. Ship's papers

2. Paper profits

3. On paper

4. Paperback

5. Paper-like cloth made from mulberry bark

6. Paperhanger

7. Paper knife

8. Paper nautilus

9. Paper wasp

10. Paperweight

11. "Paper bleeds little."

12. "Youth and white paper take any impression."

13. Papers hidden in a pumpkin

14. Curling papers for the hair

15. Flypaper

SHUCKING CORN

Not worth shucks does not mean worthless in this exercise. Every answer will yield "corn". Example: A staple food — Cornbread or corn pone.

1. Illinois, Indiana, Iowa

2. Once smoking material for adventurous boys

3. Tourist mecca in Mitchell, South Dakota

4. Kentucky

5. Nebraska

6. Irritate someone's prejudices

7. English legislation forbidding importation of grain

8. Wrestling term

9. Bachelor's buttons

10. Saying denoting plenty

11. When corn is high, beef is cheap.

12. Australian youths

13. Slang for something hackneyed or unsophisticated

14. Larva of a moth

15. Lamb's lettuce

SHUCKING CORN

1. Corn Belt

2. Corn silk

3. Corn Palace

4. Corn Cracker State

5. Cornhusker State

6. Tread on her/his corns

7. Corn Laws

8. Cornish hug

9. Cornflowers

10. There is corn in Egypt.

11. Up corn, down horn.

12. Cornstalks

13. Corny

14. Corn borer

15. Corn salad

PENNY SAVERS...

will not increase their hoard by even finding at least one "penny" in every answer. Example: A unit of troy weight — Pennyweight.

1. The prodigal returns.

2. The philosophy of saving

3. It pays to shop around.

4. Don't scorn the least bit of money.

5. Someone who skimps, then unwisely splurges

6. Arithmetic of saving

7. Don't pay for labor beforehand

8. Actress

9. Site in Canada's Northwest Territories

10. A considerable sum of money

11. Addressed to someone in a "'brown study"

12. A project started and finished despite unforeseen difficulties

13. No pay, no work

14. Old name for a freelance newspaper writer

15. Cheap boy's paper with no literary value

PENNY SAVERS

1   A bad penny always turns up.

2.   A penny saved is a penny earned.

3.   'Tis a well spent penny that saves a dollar.

4.   He who will not keep a penny shall never have many.

5.   Pennywise and pound foolish.

6.   Save and Have. A penny a day makes dollars a year.

7.   He that pays for work before it is done has but a pennyworth for two pence.

8.   Penny Marshall or Penny Singleton

9.   Penny Highland

10. A pretty penny

11. A penny for your thoughts.

12. In for a penny, in for a pound.

13. No penny, no paternoster

14. Penny-a-liner

15. Penny-dreadful

DEAD AS DEAD CAN BE

Latin, according to an old song. So why do Latin phrases infuse English as often as ketchup gives tang to a hamburger? Example: *Experto crede* — Believe one who has had experience.

1. *Ad hoc*

2. *Ad nauseam*

3. *De facto*

4. *Ergo*

5. *Ex hypothesi*

6. *Ex parte*

7. *Ex professo*

8. *In loco parentis*

9. *In toto*

10. *Modus operendi*

11. *Postmortem*

12. *Pro tempore*

13. *Semper fidelis*

14. *Status quo*

15. *Verbatim*

DEAD AS DEAD CAN BE

1. For the end or purpose at hand

2. To a sickening degree

3. In fact, though not by right

4. Therefore

5. According to what is assumed

6. Prejudiced

7. Expressly

8. In place of a parent

9. Totally

10. Method of operation

11. Analysis after an event

12. For the time being

13. Always faithful

14. Existing order of things

15. Word for word

IT WAS A DARK AND STORMY NIGHT

The wind struck with a fiendish shriek. Lightning dared the thunder to match its ferocity, and rain romped in cascades. Intermittent slashes of sleet promised snow. The man needed to find shelter quickly, — but a "storm" will overtake you in every answer.

1. One title in Winston Churchill's trilogy about World War II

2. Actress with two names that suggest violent weather

3. Certain sea birds

4. Czech proverb about bad weather

5. Retreat from violent weather

6. First military confrontation with Saddam Hussein

7. General Schwarzkopf's nickname

8. Protective devices mounted by homeowners before winter

9. Description of a woebegone person

10. Person who introduces discordant note into situation

11. Elevation of considerable mass in South Africa

12. Nazi *Sturmabteilung*

13. Mother Carey's chicken

14. Meteorological term describing approach of bad weather

15. Phrase describes serene period before upheaval

IT WAS A DARK AND STORMY NIGHT

1. *The Gathering Storm*

2. Gale Storm

3. Storm petrels

4. "Misfortune will find its way even on a dark and stormy night."

5. Storm cellar

6. Desert Storm

7. Stormin' Norman

8. Storm doors and windows

9. Like a dying duck in a thunderstorm

10. Stormy petrel

11. Stormberg Mountains

12. Storm troopers

13. A storm petrel

14. A storm front

15. The calm before a storm

LONG TIME...

means the minutes will tick away while you discover how "long" an answer can be. Example: Patiently enduring — Long-suffering.

1.   U.S. Senator assassinated in Baton Rouge

2.   American poet and college professor

3.   Communal dwelling of Iroquois Indians

4.   Virago in reign of Henry VIII

5.   Confederate army officer

6.   Collection of short stories by John Steinbeck

7.   Gist

8.   City of southwestern California

9.   Operator of system that places telephone calls

10.   Theodore Roosevelt's son-in-law

11.   Arithmetical process

12.   Paper money

13.   Cursive writing

14.   Cattle identified with southwestern United States

15.   Desire that cannot be fulfilled

LONG TIME

1.   Huey Pierce Long

2.   Henry Wadsworth Longfellow

3.   Long house

4.   Long Meg of Westminster

5.   James Longstreet

6.   *The Long Valley*

7.   The long and short of it

8.   Long Beach

9.   Long distance

10.   Nicholas Longworth

11.   Long division

12.   Long green

13.   Longhand

14.   Longhorn

15.   Longing

SAND STORM

Shakespeare said, "The sands are number'd that make up my life." These sands are not trickling through an hourglass. They are sweeping across the page to envelop you in a swirl of questions answered in some way with "sand". Example: Oil used in perfumery — Sandalwood.

1. Area in Nebraska

2. Former name for Sumba

3. Children's play site

4. Snack invented by nobleman unwilling to leave card table

5. Wading bird

6. Weapon against floodwaters

7. Hazard on a golf course

8. Captain Cook's name for the Hawaiian Islands

9. Shoe

10. Pen name of Amandine Aurore Lucie Dupin

11. Means of etching glass, or cleaning stone or metal surfaces

12. Thin, circular echinoderm

13. Advertising medium

14. Ceremonial design of Navajo Indians

15. Offshore shoal built up by waves or current

SAND STORM

1. Sand Hills

2. Sandalwood Island

3. Sandbox

4. Sandwich

5. Sandpiper

6. Sandbag

7. Sand trap

8. Sandwich Islands

9. Sandal

10. George Sand

11. Sand blast

12. Sand dollar

13. Sandwich board

14. Sand painting

15. Sandbar

COCK YOUR EYE THIS WAY

All answers contain the word "cock". Example: A tricorn — Cocked hat.

1.   A long, rambling, incredible yarn

2.   A small heap of hay thrown up temporarily

3.   Dominant bully

4.   His house will be set on fire.

5.   The third watch of a Hebrew night

6.   Favorite sport of Greeks and Romans introduced into Britain

7.   Easy to brag in your own home when unlikely to be challenged

8.   Child's play with an adult

9.   That tale won't wash.

10.   A squint

11.   Belgium

12.   Overpoweringly certain

13.   Beat someone in a contest of skills, etc.

14.   Garret

15.   Gratify one's innermost feelings

COCK YOUR EYE THIS WAY

1. A cock and bull story

2. Hay cock

3. Cock of the walk

4. The red cock will crow in his house.

5. Cock-crow

6. Cock-fighting

7. Every cock crows on its own dunghill.

8. Ride a cock-horse

9. That cock won't fight.

10. Cock-eye

11. Cock-pit of Europe

12. Cock sure

13. Knocked into a cocked hat

14. Cockloft

15. Warm the cockles of one's heart.

BLOW ME DOWN!

All answers contain the word "blow". Example: Sound a musical instrument — Blow a trumpet.

1.   Vacillate between favor and opposition

2.   Puffer

3.   Puncture of a tire's inner tube

4.   By one stroke

5.   Nostril at highest point on a whale's head

6.   To lose one's temper

7.   Flies that deposit eggs in carrion

8.   Expected end of a minor crisis

9.   A usually portable gas burner

10. A photographic enlargement

11. A braggart

12. Without coming to a contest

13. Slang for a large party or social affair

14. A metal tube in which a flow of gas is mixed with a controlled flow of gas

15. A common 18th Century name for a rustic girl

BLOW ME DOWN!

1. Blow hot and cold

2. Blowfish

3. Blowout

4. At one blow

5. Blowhole

6. Blow one's top

7. Blowflies

8. It will soon blow over.

9. Blowtorch

10. A blowup

11. Blowhard

12. Without striking a blow

13. Blowout

14. Blowpipe

15. Blowzelinda

IT'S BERRY PICKIN' TIME

It takes mental association with a berry to answer these questions.

1.   What is a color of a cow or horse?

2.   What hair color do some women favor?

3.   What is the symbol of a dukedom?

4.   What shrub or tree produces fruit used for wine or preserves?

5.   What is an exclamation question sometimes heard?

6.   What does a chaperone for lovers do?

7.   How can you show contempt?

8.   What is a dull time in journalism?

9.   How did John Greenleaf Whittier's *Barefoot Boy* receive a kiss?

10. How did Indians achieve red or pink dye?

11. What berry did Whittier recall *In School Days*?

12. How did Victorian-age ladies try to enhance their complexions?

13. What baseball star ruined his career with drugs?

14. In provincial France, what were newlyweds served as an aphrodisiac?

15. Why was Henry VIII's second wife, Anne Boleyn, considered a witch?

IT'S BERRY PICKIN' TIME

1. Strawberry roan

2. Strawberry blonde

3. Six strawberry leaves

4. Elderberry

5. "Isn't that the berries!"

6. Play gooseberry

7. Give a raspberry

8. The big gooseberry season

9. "...strawberries on the hill"

10. Rubbed cloth with strawberries to desired color

11. Blackberry

12. Masks of crushed strawberries

13. Daryl Strawberry

14. Soup of thinned sour cream, strawberries, borage (a European herb with a flavor like cucumber) and powdered sugar

15. She had a strawberry-shaped birthmark on her neck.

WHEN LENT IS NOT *THE* LENT

Galeazzo's Lent was a form of torture devised by a Duke of Milan to prolong the unfortunate victim's life for 40 days. This exercise is not meant to be torture, and it has no religious significance. Lent's four letters merely are contained in each answer. Example: Pompous in speech or behavior — Flatulent.

1. Exhibiting conflicting feelings or thoughts

2. Obese

3. Expulsive

4. Deceitful

5. Lazy

6. Audaciously impudent

7. Music: Slow

8. Malicious

9. Deadly

10. Common

11. Pleasantly odorous

12. Repulsive

13. Cactus

14. Savage and cruel

15. Severe

WHEN LENT IS NOT *THE* LENT

1.   Ambivalent

2.   Corpulent.

3.   Expellent

4.   Fraudulent

5.   Indolent

6.   Insolent

7.   *Lento*

8.   Malevolent

9.   Pestilent

10.   Prevalent

11.   Redolent

12.   Repellent

13.   Succulent

14.   Truculent

15.   Violent

KNOW PASSING ZONE

All answers contain "know". Example: Proverb about caution in buying — "Don't throw away the old bucket until you know if the new one holds water."

1.   Book authored by Robert Fulghum

2.   Poem by Louis C. Shimon

3.   Admonition of the oracle of Apollo at Delphi

4.   Doubt of women's ability to keep a secret

5.   Poem by Nixon Waterman

6.   Secret 19th Century political society in U.S.

7.   Tool that can be used to change and control the world

8.   Poem by Mary Carolyn Davies

9.   Proverb about a quick lesson in finance

10.   Said of a dullard

11.   Poem by Holly Carrington Brent

12.   Said to be an aid in climbing the ladder of success

13.   Experienced person in any area of activity

14.   Difference between a bird and a man

15.   Be aware

KNOW PASSING ZONE

1. *All I Really Need To Know I Learned in Kindergarten*

2. *I Know Something Good About You*

3. "Know Thyself."

4. "Women will keep silent only those things they do not know."

5. *To Know All Is To Forgive All*

6. Know-Nothings

7. Knowledge is power.

8. *If I Had Known*

9. "Would you know the value of money, go and borrow some."

10. Doesn't know beans

11. *I Think I Know No Finer Things Than Dogs*

12. Know the right people.

13. Know the ropes.

14. A bird is known by its note; a man by his talk.

15. In the know

15 GATES

According to the Arabian, what we say must pass Three Gates? Is it true? Is it needful? Is it kind?
You have your hands on the latches of 15 gates. No crannied walls — these. Every word defined has a gate, and you can pass through without offending anyone.

1. Abolish or annul by authority

2. Trifle

3. Gather

4. Authorized representative

5. Controls the flow of a body of water

6. Exterminate vermin or insects

7. Official emissary

8. To engage in legal proceedings

9. Moderate

10. To bind by a legal or moral tie

11. Given over to dissipation

12. Consign to an obscure place

13. Substitute

14. To follow another vehicle too closely

15. Restrain a flood

15 GATES

1.   Abrogate

2.   Bagatelle

3.   Congregate

4.   Delegate

5.   Floodgate

6.   Fumigate

7.   Legate

8.   Litigate

9.   Mitigate

10.   Obligate

11.   Profligate

12.   Relegate

13.   Surrogate

14.   Tailgate

15.   Watergate

WHEN WORDS MEET THE GUILLOTINE

If you remove the first letter of one word for ......, it leaves another word for ...... Example: Christian love, stare wonderingly — Agape, gape.

1. Disconcert, strike a crushing blow

2. A store of goods hidden, pain

3. Exposure to harm, ire

4. Dishearten, expel

5. Occurrence, exit

6. Starve, sect

7. Object of prolonged endeavor, marsh bird

8. Position of leadership, tree

9. Principal structural member of a ship, fish

10. Servant, help

11. Combat with lances, force out

12. Game to break a tie, temporary unemployment

13. Decoy, elevated area

14. Black, capable

15. Flounder, permit

WHEN WORDS MEET THE GUILLOTINE

1.   Abash, bash

2.   Cache, ache

3.   Danger, anger

4.   Deject, eject

5.   Event, vent

6.   Famish, Amish

7.   Grail, rail

8.   Helm, elm

9.   Keel, eel

10.   Maid, aid.

11.   Joust, oust

12.   Playoff, layoff

13.   Shill, hill

14.   Sable, able

15.   Wallow, allow

WITH THESE RINGS, I THEE TRY TO CONFOUND

A ring has multiple definitions. Its uses are captured in this quiz as adjective, noun or verb. All answers contain "ring". Example: Novel by Danielle Steel — *The Ring.*

1.   Tale that made movie history

2.   Used by the Pope to seal papal briefs

3.   Moving spirit of an enterprise, usually of a mutinous character

4.   To outclass someone easily

5.   A long poem by Robert Browning

6.   Circlet in Westminster Abbey, once given to beggar, later returned from Holy Land by man who claimed to be John the Evangelist

7.   Child's game

8.   Has intrinsic merit

9.   Producing continual changes on a set of bells without repetition

10.   Line of marriage service

11.   End a telephone conversation

12.   A series of four operas by Richard Wagner

13.   Rouse a memory

14.   Game bird

15.   A horseshoe or quoit thrown so that it encircles peg

WITH THESE RINGS, I THEE TRY TO CONFOUND

1.   *The Lord of the Rings*

2.   Ring of the Fisherman

3.   Ringleader

4.   Run rings around

5.   *The Ring and The Book*

6.   Ring of Edward the Confessor

7.   Ring Around the Rosy

8.   It has the true ring.

9.   Ringing the changes

10.   With this ring, I thee wed.

11.   Ring off

12.   *Der Ring des Nibelungen*

13.   Ring a bell

14.   Ring-necked pheasant

15.   Ringer

BECAUSE IT IS *GOOD* FOR YOU

That's the message from well-meaning people who urge you to eat cilantro, or run four miles in one minute. A task half-heartedly completed hopefully is "*good* enough," and the "*good* guys" always win. It's your turn to find the positive-sounding four-letter word.

1. Virtually

2. Entirely

3. Able to continue

4. Worthless

5. Bad end

6. For all time

7. To one's benefit

8. A person of little worth

9. Thirty miles south of Gape Town, South Africa

10. Attractive

11. Promotion by President Franklin D. Roosevelt of friendly economic and political relations between United States and Latin America

12. Compassionate person who helps others

13. Friendliness

14. American inventor of vulcanized rubber

15. Cloyingly sanctimonious

BECAUSE IT IS *GOOD* FOR YOU

1. As good as

2. Good and

3. Good for

4. No good

5. Come to no good

6. For good

7. To the good

8. Good-for-nothing

9. Cape of Good Hope

10. Good looking

11. Good Neighbor Policy

12. Good Samaritan

13. Good will

14. Charles Goodyear

15. Goody-goody

TALKING ABOUT THE NEIGHBORS

1. What French explorer is generally regarded as founder of Canada?

2. What English explorer had sighted Newfoundland late in the 15th Century?

3. Who probably explored Canada centuries earlier?

4. What present-day phenomenon suggests this exploration?

5. Who reached the Pacific, and inscribed a rock, "From Canada by land"?

6. Where was most of America's War of 1812 fought?

7. Who were the British and French generals mortally wounded in a battle on the Plains of Abraham near Quebec?

8. Who defeated whom?

9. Evangeline and all the other inhabitants were expelled from what area by order of George II?

10. What do we call that province today?

11. What is the capital of Canada?

12. Name the 12 provinces / territories of Canada.

13. What French-speaking province would like to separate itself from the rest of Canada?

14. What event of May 28, 1934, enthralled the world for years?

15. What area attracted a gold rush?

TALKING ABOUT THE NEIGHBORS

1. Jacques Cartier

2. John Cabot

3. Vikings

4. Blue-eyed Indians

5. Sir Alexander Mackenzie

6. Upper Canada

7. James Wolfe and Louis Joseph Marquis de Montcalm de Saint-Veran

8. General Wolfe

9. Acadia

10. Nova Scotia

11. Ottawa

12. Alberta, British Columbia, Manitoba, New Brunswick, Newfoundland, Nova Scotia, Ontario, Prince Edward Island, Quebec, Saskatchewan, Northwest Territories, Yukon Territory

13. Quebec

14. Birth of Dionne Quintuplets

15. Klondike in Yukon Territory

STILL TALKING ABOUT THE NEIGHBORS

1. Who built immense stone pyramids in Mexico, and invented a calendar?

2. Who destroyed the Aztec empire?

3. Who were the French-supported puppet emperor and empress of Mexico?

4. Who was responsible for the emperor's execution?

5. What Mexican president seized the Alamo?

6. Outnumbered 4-1, who defeated the Mexicans at Buena Vista?

7. What Mexican brigand incensed Americans prior to World War I?

8. What diplomat was captivated by a Mexican shrub destined to become an American holiday favorite?

9. What is the plant?

10. How many states does Mexico have?

11. What is the capital of Mexico?

12. What is the national anthem of Mexico?

13. What is the Mexican monetary unit?

14. How is a U.S.-Mexican trade agreement known?

15. What river separates the United States and Mexico?

STILL TALKING ABOUT THE NEIGHBORS

1. Mayas

2. Hernando Cortez

3. Maximilian and Carlotta

4. Benito Juarez

5. Santa Anna, Antonio Lopez de

6. Zachary Taylor

7. Poncho Villa

8. John Poinsett

9. Poinsettia

10. 31 States, 1 federal district

11. Mexico City

12. *Mexicanos al grito guerre*

13. New peso

14. NAFTA

15. Rio Grande

IDENTICAL TWINS...

appear in the English language, too. Example: Something forbidden — No-no. Keep going. Fifteen chances to challenge you remain.

1. Thiamine deficiency disease of the peripheral nervous system

2. Candy with fondant center, fruit or nuts

3. Farewell

4. One who is overwhelmingly sanctimonious

5. Silly

6. Hawaiian dress

7. Neither very good nor very bad

8. Small-headed drum beaten with hands

9. Spool around which a string is wound

10. Anti-aircraft fire

11. A standard size of lead shot

12. Mistake

13. Dance

14. Extinct bird, or a person hopelessly antiquated

15. Lively in the manner of modem youth

IDENTICAL TWINS

1. Beri-beri

2. Bon-bon

3. Bye-bye

4. Goody-goody

5. Ga-ga

6. Muu-muu

7. So-so

8. Tom-tom

9. Yo-yo

10. Ack-ack

11. B.B.

12. Boo-boo

13. Can-can

14. Do-do

15. Go-go

FRATERNAL TWINS...

are words, too. At least, our language use has given then an affinity for each other. Example: Predecessor of cell phone — Walkie-talkie.

1.   Small talk

2.   Ice cream containing variety of chopped, candied fruit

3.   Disembowelment

4.   Used to express mild annoyance

5.   Jitters

6.   Chinese salutation

7.   Possibly insincere show of friendship

8.   Cutesy description of smallness

9.   Disorder

10.   A swindle

11.   Disorderly haste

12.   Uneasiness

13.   Pretentious language

14.   Rapid series of light tapping sounds

15.   Whether desired or not

FRATERNAL TWINS

1. Chit-chat

2. Tutti-frutti

3. *Hari-kari*

4. Fiddle-faddle

5. Jim-jams

6. Kow-tow

7. Palsy-walsy

8. Itsy-bitsy

9. Hurly-burly

10. Flim-flam

11. Pell-mell, helter-skelter, hurry-scurry

12. Heebie-jeebies

13. Clap-trap

14. Pitter-patter

15. Willy-nilly

FOR LAND'S SAKE!

Land, lots of land —— and not a fence in sight. All answers contain the word "land". Example: An aircraft runway without airport facilities — Landing strip.

1. Overwhelming triumph at polls

2. Signal to Paul Revere

3. A government transfer of public property for a railroad, highway or state college

4. Inventor of Polaroid products

5. Whether conditions are propitious

6. The sighting or reaching of land on a voyage or flight

7. Surrounded or nearly surrounded by land

8. Man/woman who owns and rents real estate

9. Undercarriage of an aircraft, designed to support weight of craft and its load on ground.

10. Explosive device

11. A person unfamiliar with sea or seamanship

12. A building or site having special significance

13. A country scene, or a picture representing this

14. Informal, sleep

15. Minnesota

FOR LAND'S SAKE!

1. Landslide

2. One, if by land; two, if by sea.

3. Land grant

4. Edwin Herbert Land

5. See how the land lies.

6. Landfall

7. Landlocked

8. Landlord/landlady

9. Landing gear

10. Land mine

11. Landlubber

12. Landmark

13. Landscape

14. Land of Nod

15. Land of Sky Blue Waters

TOMALLEY...

is the liver of a lobster, but you'll find the emphasis on "tom" in every answer to the clues that follow.

1. River in the former Soviet Union

2. Tool or weapon used by American Indians

3. He stole a pig, and away he run.

4. Hot rum drink

5. Copper and zinc alloy used in inexpensive jewelry

6. Astronomer who discovered planet Pluto

7. River rising in Mississippi, and flowing 500 miles to Mobile River

8. Young girl who behaves like a spirited boy

9. Male feline

10. Beverage said to be named for bartender who invented it

11. Silly behavior

12. British expression for provisions

13. British soldier

14. Submachine-gun

15. Nonsense

TOMALLEY

1. Tom

2. Tomahawk

3. Tom, Tom, the Piper's Son

4. Tom and Jerry

5. Tombac

6. Clyde William Tombaugh

7. Tombigbee

8. Tomboy

9. Tomcat

10. Tom Collins

11. Tomfoolery

12. Tommy

13. Tommy Atkins

14. Tommy gun

15. Tommyrot

FROM RAGS TO RICHES

The answer to the first part of this exercise contain the word "rag". Example: Anger — rage. The second section concerns people who are "rich" through an accident of name. Example: Composer of *South Pacific* — Richard Rodgers.

1.   Easily broken

2.   Cucumber-flavored seasoning

3.   Below legal age

4.   Babble

5.   Scent

6.   Active rather than contemplative

7.   Benefice of a vicar

8.   Overwhelming, concentrated outpouring of words or blows

9.   Disastrous event

10. Optical phenomenon

11. Meat and vegetable stew

12. A scold

13. Former Speaker of the House

14. Black novelist, short story writer

15. Survived three months adrift in Pacific

FROM RAGS TO RICHES

1. Fragile

2. Borage

3. Underage

4. Ragtag

5. Fragrance

6. Pragmatic

7. Vicarage

8. Barrage

9. Tragedy

10. Mirage

11. Ragout

12. Virago

13. Newt Gingrich

14. Richard Wright

15. Richard Van Pham

MORNING, NOON AND NIGHT...

sounds stressful when we hear someone say it. In this quiz, the times of day are separate entities — in order, 7 mornings, 3 noons and 5 nights.

1. General George Custer

2. Often Venus

3. Flowering vine

4. Matins

5. Song composed by Walter Donaldson

6. Lord Byron's name for Mary Chaworth with whom he once was in love

7. 1933 Movie for which Katherine Hepburn won the Academy Award

8. Movie that won an Oscar for Gary Cooper in 1952

9. Poetic reference to mid-day

10. Middle of the day sound in small towns

11. Movie that swept the Academy Awards in 1934

12. Song that sometimes ends a gala evening celebration

13. Cole Porter classic

14. Drama by Robert E. Sherwood

15. Napoleon Bonaparte

MORNING, NOON AND NIGHT

1. Son of the Morning Star

2. Morning Sun

3. Morning-glory

4. Morning Prayer

5. *Carolina in the Morning*

6. The Morning Star

7. *Morning Glory*

8. *High Noon*

9. Noontide

10. Noon whistle

11. *It Happened One Night*

12. *Good Night, Ladies*

13. *Night and Day*

14. *There Shall Be No Night*

15. Nightmare of Europe

IT MUST BE SOMETHING IN THE WATER

All answers contain the word "water". It may be a proverb, a definition, a title or the name of a person with an outstanding achievement. Example: Blues singer, songwriter — Muddy Waters.

1.   Relationship has a claim.

2.   Fair, but empty words

3.   I am a Jack of all trades.

4.   In trouble

5.   Scandal that ended a presidency

6.   Of the highest type

7.   Deep thinkers are persons of few words.

8.   Mississippi river

9.   Test for adultery in Biblical times

10.   Retract

11.   Carry coals to Newcastle

12.   Seek to turn a disturbance to one's own advantage

13.   Discourage a proposal

14.   Cry, blubber

15.   A design impressed into paper in the course of manufacture

IT MUST BE SOMETHING IN THE WATER

1. Blood is thicker than water.

2. Court holy water.

3. I am for all waters.

4. In hot water

5. Watergate

6. Of the first water

7. Still waters run deep.

8. Father of Waters

9. The water of jealousy

10. Back water

11. Carry water to the river

12. Fish in troubled waters

13. Throw cold water on a scheme

14. Turn on the waterworks

15. Watermark

THE LONG-EARED FRATERNITY

Jesus rode an ass in His triumphal entry into Jerusalem. A prospector may have a string of burros. This exercise explores how much-maligned animals have colored our language. Example: sanctuary for a revolver — Mule-ear holster.

1. A proverb very like the one that a leopard cannot change its spots

2. A proverb like the pot calling the kettle black

3. A proverb about not taking responsibility

4. A proverb about a traveler's strengths

5. Child's game

6. Animal-human sport

7. A small auxiliary steam engine

8. Not for a long time

9. Different people see from different viewpoints.

10. To be pig-headed

11. An old cry at fairs

12. An old gibe against police officers

13. Never

14. A coward who hectors

15. To do something very foolish

THE LONG-EARED FRATERNITY

1. "A donkey laden with gold is still a donkey."

2. "Nothing is gained by having one donkey call another "long ears."

3. "It is a sorry donkey that will not bear his own burden."

4. A traveler should have a hog's nose, a deer's legs and a donkey's back.

5. Pin the tail on the donkey.

6. Donkey basketball.

7. Donkey engine.

8. Not for donkey's years.

9. The donkey means one thing, and the driver another.

10. To ride the black donkey.

11. Two more, and up goes the donkey.

12. Who stole the donkey?

13. Till the ass ascends the ladder.

14. An ass in a lion's skin.

15. To make an ass of oneself.

UP FOR AIR

It's colorless, odorless, tasteless, approximately 78 percent nitrogen and 21 percent oxygen, but we can't get along without it, even in our language. All answers contain the word "air".

1.   What movie won an Academy Award for Helen Hayes in 1970?

2.   Affectation

3.   Feel elated

4.   Being broadcast by radio or television

5.   Angry

6.   Home turf for certain military personnel

7.   Swamp craft

8.   Mary Stewart novel plotted around Lippanzer horses

9.   Delivery of supplies or troops by parachute

10.   Large terrier developed in England

11.   Atomizer to spray paint

12.   Cooling system

13.   Protective use of military planes

14.   River in western Yorkshire, England

15.   Large ship used as mobile base

UP FOR AIR

1.   *Airport*

2.   Give oneself airs

3.   Walk on air

4.   On the air

5.   Up in the air

6.   Air base

7.   Air boat

8.   *Airs Above the Ground*

9.   Air drop

10.   Airedale

11.   Air brush

12.   Air conditioning

13.   Air cover

14.   Aire

15.   Aircraft carrier

GO-GO

Answers to the first segment of this exercise *begin* with "go". Concluding answers *end* in go". Examples: A young goose — gosling; friend — *amigo*.

1. Drinking glass with base and stem

2. Haunting ghost

3. Intentional slight

4. Small wagon for children

5. Enterprising, hustling person

6. Persian pottery

7. Slang for one who is ruined or doomed

8. Rust

9. Tropical fruit

10. Any prohibitions

11. A painful, inflammatory rheumatism

12. Dialect

13. Animated Spanish-American dance in triple time

14. Dizziness

15. Wild dog

GO-GO

1. Goblet

2. Goblin

3. Go-by

4. Go-cart

5. Go-getter

6. Gombroon

7. Goner

8. Aerugo

9. Mango

10. Embargo

11. Lumbago

12. Lingo

13. Fandango

14. Vertigo

15. Dingo

THREE OUTS...

and you're still at bat. All exercise answers are "outs". Example: Detachable engine for a boat — Outboard motor.

1. Playing area extending from baseball diamond

2. Strong protest

3. Extroverted

4. Bizarre

5. Habitual criminal

6. Disbursement of money

7. Temporary suspension of electric power

8. Point of view

9. Old-fashioned

10. Seagoing canoe

11. Surpass in cleverness

12. Relieved from distress or danger

13. The secret is bound to be revealed.

14. Expenditure

15. Incomparably

THREE OUTS

1. Outfield

2. Outcry

3. Outgoing

4. Outlandish

5. Outlaw

6. Outlay

7. Outage

8. Outlook

9. Out-of-date

10. Outrigger

11. Outwit

12. Out from under

13. Murder will out

14. Out of pocket

15. Out and out

YOU CAN SAY THAT AGAIN

A business college instructor urged students to always begin letters with "You" because everyone is primarily interested in self. Below are the meanings of 15 proverbs, or sayings, all of which begin with "You". Example: Glorified memories of the past — You can't go home again.

1. There's always a price to pay.

2. Ups and downs of life

3. Purchasing power

4. Learning the ropes

5. Decisions, decisions!

6. When it's impossible to challenge someone

7. The best is yet to come.

8. When creative ability falters

9. Failures are part of everyone's life.

10. You do me a favor; I'll reciprocate.

11. Careful expenditure

12. Silence

13. Your body reflects your food intake

14. Being a motor-mouth

15. A monetary reward is preferred.

YOU CAN SAY THAT AGAIN

1.	You can't get something for nothing.

2.	You have to take the bad with the good.

3.	You pays your money, and you takes your choice.

4.	You have to learn to walk before you can run.

5.	You can't have it both ways.

6.	You can't argue with success.

7.	You ain't seen nothin' yet.

8.	You can't make a silk purse out of a sow's ear.

9.	You can't win 'em all.

10.	You scratch my back; I'll scratch yours.

11.	You get what you pay for.

12.	You could hear a pin drop.

13.	You are what you eat.

14.	You may talk too much on the best of subjects.

15.	You can't put Thanks in your pocket.

MEN OF OUR BATTLE YEARS

Listed, are some of the men identified with the nation's wars. Note his role and war. Example: Billy Mitchell, air power advocate, World War I.

1.   Creighton Abrams

2.   Henry "Hap" Arnold

3.   Pierre Beauregard

4.   Edward Braddock

5.   Claire Lee Chennault

6.   George Armstrong Custer

7.   George Dewey

8.   Dwight D. Eisenhower

9.   David Farragut

10.   Tommy Franks

11.   Ulysses S. &rant

12.   Nathanael Greene

13.   Isaac Hull

14.   Stephen Kearny

15.   Robert E. Lee

MEN OF OUR BATTLE YEARS

1.   Commander, Vietnam

2.   Army Air Fore Commander, World War II

3.   Confederate general, Civil War

4.   Commander, French and Indian War

5.   Headed Flying Tigers, World War II

6.   Commander at Battle of Little Big Horn

7.   Destroyed Spanish fleet, Spanish-American War

8.   Supreme Commander, European theater, World War II

9.   Union Admiral, Civil War

10. General, Iraqi Freedom War

11. Union General, Civil War

12. General, American Revolution

13. Sank British frigate, War of 1812

14. Headed Army of the West, Mexican War

15. Confederate general, Civil War

AS DOES THE LARK

It's said that a lark spirals into the sky for a word with God. Possibly persons with a sky to their names have a leg up on reaching the heights, even if a name is changed to a more prosaic designation. You have a chance to learn how the following men and women fared. Example: Walter Matthau — Walter Matuschanskayasky.

1.   World-renowned printmaker. Argentine-born

2.   Russian chess player, journalist

3.   Movie director (*Harry and Tonto*)

4.   Mike Nichols who won an Academy Award for *The Graduate*

5.   Singer (*On the Wings of a Dove*)

6.   Russian abstractionist

7.   Russian who headed provisional government after 1917 revolution

8.   Russian revolutionary, founded Red party

9.   Writer born in Long Branch, New Jersey

10.   Poet, won 1987 Nobel prize for literature

11.   Author of *Remembering Mog*

12.   Jack Benny

13.   Mel Brooks

14.   Danny Kaye

15.   Joan Rivers

AS DOES THE LARK

1. Mauricio Lasansky

2. Boris Spassky

3. Paul Mazursky

4. Michael Igor Peschkowsky

5. Ferlin Husky

6. Vasily Kandinsky

7. Aleksandr Kerensky

8. Leon Trotsky

9. Robert Pinsky

10. Joseph Brodsky

11. Colby Rodowsky

12. Benjamin Kubelsky

13. Melvin Kaminsky

14. David Kaminsky

15. Joan Sandra Molinsky

SIGNS OF RAIN

It is said that into every life some rain must fall. You receive an undue amount of precipitation in this exercise. "Rain" falls in every answer. Example: Novel by Ross Lockridge, Jr. — *Raintree County.*

1.   Regardless of the weather

2.   Precipitation in great quantity

3.   Song's advice about an umbrella's use

4.   Nature's postponement of an event

5.   Token of postponement

6.   Composition by Burt Bacharach

7.   Formerly Mount Tacoma

8.   Waterproof clothing

9.   Song written by Nacio Herb Brown

10.   Lake partly in Minnesota, partly in Ontario

11.   North American food fish

12.   Johnny Mercer was the lyricist for this song

13.   Lyrics by Bob Merrill

14.   Movie and male star won Oscars in 1988

15.   Respected figure among American Indians

SIGNS OF RAIN

1. Rain or shine

2. Rain cats and dogs

3. *Let A Smile Be Your Umbrella on A Rainy, Rainy Day*

4. Rain out

5. Rain check

6. *Raindrops Keep Fallin' on my Head*

7. Mount Rainier

8. Rainwear

9. *Singing in the Rain*

10. Rainy Lake

11. Rainbow trout

12. *Come Rain or Come Shine*

13. *Don't Rain on my Parade*

14. *Rain Man*

15. Rainmaker

HAND WORK

No knitting, nor crocheting. Only give a hand to every answer.

1.   Apprehension in perpetration of crime

2.   Possession is better than expectation.

3.   You must not expect to receive anything without giving a return.

4.   Wild Bill Hickok's last game of cards

5.   A promise to pay made in writing

6.   In friendly fashion

7.   One who is experienced

8.   To pass from one owner to another

9.   An unskilled person

10.   I am totally occupied.

11.   Obtain the mastery

12.   Nautical term for a ship's crew

13.   Conveniently near

14.   Me

15.   Order given by robbers or other captors

HAND WORK

1. Caught red-handed

2. A bird in the hand is better than two in the bush.

3. An empty hand is no lure for a hawk.

4. Dead man's hand

5. A note of hand

6. Hand in hand

7. An old hand

8. To change hands

9. A poor hand

10. My hands are full.

11. Get the upper hand

12. All hands

13. At hand

14. To hand in one's checks

15. Hands up!

JULY 4TH QUIZ

Hats off!
Along the street there comes
A blare of bugles, a ruffle of drums,
A flash of color beneath the sky.
Hats off!
The flag is passing by.

1. Who wrote *The Flag Goes By?*

2. What date did John Adams think would be the most memorable in American history?

3. What occurred on that date?

4. What occurred two days later?

5. At least a dozen flags preceded the U.S. flag we know today. Name two of them.

6. Who designed the final American flag?

7. Who put forward Betsy Ross' claim to being the seamstress who made the first official flag?

8. When?

9. How was the announcement publicized?

10. Who first called the U.S. flag Old Glory?

11. When?

12. When did the number of stripes cease to increase?

13. When is a new star added?

14. What two founding fathers died on July 4?

15. What President was born on July 4?

JULY 4TH QUIZ

1. Henry Holcomb Bennett

2. July 2

3. The Continental Congress ratified its decision to secede from England.

4. The founding fathers adopted the Declaration of Independence.

5. First Navy Jack, Philadelphia Light Horse Flag, Grand Union Flag, Bunker Hill Flag, First Stars and Stripes, Rhode Island Flag, Bennington Flag, Washington's Cruisers Flag, Ft. McHenry Flag, etc.

6. No one knows for sure. Francis Hopkinson declared he did, but Congress refused to reimburse him.

7. Her grandson, William Canby

8. Mid-1870s

9. A man who had a tavern in the former Ross home posted a sign in his bar, "The Home of the First American Flag".

10. According to his daughter, William Driver, a sea captain. His mother gave him a homemade flag for his 21st birthday.

11. March 17, 1824

12. July 4, 1818

13. On July 4 after the state is admitted

14. John Adams and Thomas Jefferson, 1826, the 50th anniversary of the Declaration of Independence

15. Calvin Coolidge

COLD WORDS FOR COMFORT

POINT BARROW, Alaska — A killer blizzard struck without warning this morning, and a state of emergency has been declared. Snow is falling at the rate of 60 inches an hour. All dog sled and snowmobile traffic has been halted by whiteouts and suddenly shifting glaciers. No thermometer has a figure low enough to register the temperature, and the wind chill is below human comprehension. A keening wind may blow the 49th state back to Russia.

Even some words either are frosted with ice, or have a shard embedded. Example: Oregano — spice.

1.   Information-opinion

2.   Vestment

3.   Beginner

4.   Trickery

5.   Truce

6.   Guidance

7.   Greed

8.   Rectory

9.   Rectitude in dealing with others

10.   Whim

11.   Goblet

12.   Rodents

13.   Cravenness

14.   Chink

15.   Interweaving strands

COLD WORDS FOR COMFORT

1.   Advice

2.   Surplice

3.   Novice

4.   Artifice

5.   Armistice

6.   Auspices

7.   Avarice

8.   Benifice

9.   Justice

10.   Caprice

11.   Chalice

12.   Mice

13.   Cowardice

14.   Crevice

15.   Splice

LITTLE BY LITTLE...

every answer in this exercise will yield its "little". Example: Dovekie, a small black and white sea bird. — Little auk.

1.   Proverb about ambition and success

2.   Scottish proverb

3.   Napoleon

4.   Faction in Swift's *Gulliver's Travels*

5.   Male nursery rhyme character

6.   Semi-legendary character in Robin Hood saga

7.   Possibly the first girl to meet a wolf

8.   Rhode Island

9.   The mole that caused William III's horse to stumble and throw him

10.   Stephen A. Douglas

11.   Czar of Russia

12.   One of John Hay's *Pike County Ballads*

13.   Site of Custer's Massacre

14.   Novel by Charles Dickens

15.   Character in *Uncle Tom's Cabin*

LITTLE BY LITTLE

1.	"From little acorns grow mighty oaks."

2.	"Many a little makes a mickle."

3.	Little Corporal

4.	Little Endions

5.	Little Boy Blue or Little Jack Horner

6.	Little John

7.	Little Red Riding Hood

8.	Little Rhody

9.	Little Gentleman in Velvet

10.	Little Giant

11.	Little Father

12.	Little Breeches

13.	Little Big Horn

14.	*Little Dorrit*

15.	Little Eva

NO WAR FOR OIL

You won't embark for the Middle East or Venezuela. No one will darkly hint that you have terrorist sympathies if you drive an SUV, or call you part of an "axis of evil". Neither will you become wealthy, but you have 15 chances to discover oil.

1.   Insincere flattery

2.   Gain sudden wealth

3.   Guacharo

4.   Heating unit

5.   Cattle feed or fertilizer

6.   Cover for tables or shelving

7.   An area with reserves of recoverable petroleum

8.   Bottom of a crankcase

9.   Refined turpentine

10.   Unctuous

11.   Sulfuric acid

12.   Municipality in Pennsylvania

13.   Tanker

14.   Waterproof garment

15.   Art

NO WAR FOR OIL

1. Oil

2. Strike oil

3. Oil bird

4. Oil burner

5. Oil cake

6. Oilcloth

7. Oil field

8. Oil pan

9. Oil of turpentine

10. Oily

11. Oil of vitriol

12. Oil City

13. Oiler

14. Oilskin

15. Oil painting

ASHES TO ASHES

According to legend, an Arabian bird, the phoenix, supposedly lives a certain number of years, builds a nest of spices, sings a lovely dirge, flaps its wings to ignite the nest, and is reduced to ashes, only to spring into new life. Today, ashes symbolize penitence — or ruin. All answers to the following questions contain an "ash", intended to affirm life. Example: Actress — Elizabeth Ashley.

1. Labor economist who helped form AFL-CIO.

2. Detective storywriter

3. Poet of light verse

4. Member of George W. Bush cabinet

5. Lyricist

6. Tree of the genus *Fraxinus*

7. Slang for a depth charge

8. A square block of building stone

9. Box elder

10. Lake in North Dakota

11. Reef in Indonesia

12. Heroine of Longfellow's poetical romance *Hyperion*

13. Negotiated by Daniel Webster to settle Maine-Canada boundary dispute

14. River in Jordan

15. Lake in Newfoundland, Canada

ASHES TO ASHES

1. Jack Barbash

2. Dashiell Hammett

3. Ogden Nash

4. John Ashcroft

5. Howard Ashman

6. Ash

7. Ash can

8. Ashlar

9. Ash-leafed maple

10. Ashabula

11. Ashmore

12. Mary Ashburton

13. Ashburton Treaty

14. Ash Shidiyah

15. Ashuanipi

WITH THESE RATES...

you can't go wrong. All the one-word answers contain "rate". Examples: Focus — Concentrate.

1. Increase speed

2. Feel or express sorrow

3. Thoughtful

4. Draw moisture from

5. Baffle or thwart

6. Thankful

7. To combine with water

8. Ungrateful person

9. Repeat

10. Fertilizer

11. Pierce

12. Commit

13. Preserve by chilling

14. Set or keep apart

15. Mild

WITH THESE RATES

1. Accelerate

2. Commiserate

3. Considerate

4. Evaporate

5. Frustrate

6. Grateful

7. Hydrate

8. Ingrate

9. Iterate

10. Nitrate

11. Penetrate

12. Perpetrate

13. Refrigerate

14. Separate

15. Temperate

BIRDS INCOGNITO

Scientists seized upon Latin to name birds. Laymen labeled them thusly for a variety of reasons. Now, for pure fun, birds are feathered in new plumage to elude easy identification. Example: Indian tribe — Crow.

1. Prince in Catholic Church

2. Slay Bambi

3. Quarrel and row

4. A stormy night

5. Grieving one

6. Peddle wares by crying in street

7. Constellation *Columba*

8. Puck's first name when using his alias

9. A member of the British Women's Royal Naval Service

10. Island group

11. Symbol of wisdom

12. Four and twenty of them were baked in a pie.

13. Maeterlinck's fancy

14. Grassland spree

15. Cute girl facing a Scotland river

BIRDS INCOGNITO

1. Cardinal

2. Killdeer

3. Sparrow

4. Nightingale

5. Mourning dove

6. Hawk

7. Dove

8. Robin

9. Wren

10. Canary

11. Owl

12. Blackbirds

13. Bluebird (of Happiness)

14. Meadow lark

15. Chickadee

IF THAT DOESN'T BEAT THE DUTCH!

Possibly because of England's struggle against The Netherlands for supremacy of the seas in the 17th Century, "Dutch" sometimes has a less than flattering definition. An effort has been made to avoid insults in this quiz, although humor may lurk. Example: Cane frame used in Indonesia in hot weather to rest arms and legs while trying to keep cool in bed.— Dutch wife. All answers contain "Dutch".

1. Open sale with a high price, and lower it until item is sold.

2. Kalimantan

3. Cottage cheese

4. White clover

5. Means of entry divided in half horizontally

6. Indonesia

7. Hastens demise of certain trees

8. Surinam

9. Spring wildflower

10. Woody vine of the eastern United States

11. Alloy of copper and zinc used as a cheap imitation of gold leaf

12. West Irian

13. Heavy pot with a tight lid, used in slow cooking

14. An outing for which each participant pays own expenses

15. A stern and candid critic

IF THAT DOESN'T BEAT THE DUTCH!

1. Dutch auction

2. Formerly Dutch Borneo

3. Dutch cheese

4. Dutch clover

5. Dutch door

6. Formerly Dutch East Indies

7. Dutch elm disease

8. Formerly Dutch Guiana

9. Dutchman's breeches

10. Dutchman's pipe

11. Dutch metal

12. Formerly Dutch New Guinea

13. Dutch oven

14. Dutch treat

15. Dutch uncle

TRY, TRY AGAIN...

for the right answers. All contain "try". Examples: Stressful — trying. High school math — Geometry. "When bad be your prospects, don't sit still and cry. Instead, jump up, and say to yourself, "I'll try."

1. Theft

2. Chivalrous attention toward women

3. Agreement between lovers about a meeting

4. High social position

5. Profession

6. Ability, quality or workmanship

7. Rural area; nation

8. Adjunct of a kitchen

9. Faulty reasoning

10. Foot soldiers

11. Management of wooded land

12. Door

13. Reckless mischief

14. Beauty as a result of balance or harmonious arrangement

15. Attention to detail or rules

TRY, TRY AGAIN

1. Banditry

2. Gallantry

3. Tryst

4. Gentry

5. Ministry

6. Artistry

7. Country

8. Pantry

9. Sophistry

10. Infantry

11. Forestry

12. Entry

13. Deviltry

14. Symmetry

15. Pedantry

AFRAID OF THE DARK

Let there be light. Early answers in this exercise are "dark". "Light" shines in the remainder. Examples: Cross a threshold — Darken one's door. Poem by Francis W. Bourdillon — *Light*.

1. Newbery Medal Book by Charles Boardman Hawes

2. Martin Flavin's Pulitzer Prize Book

3. Era following death of Charlemagne

4. Translation of Indian name for Kentucky

5. Africa

6. Person whose abilities are untried

7. Novel by John Galsworthy

8. Mysterious person to whom Shakespeare addressed poetry

9. Novel by Sherwood Anderson

10. Play by George Bernard Shaw

11. A step the consequences of which cannot be foreseen

12. When things have come to their worst, they must mend.

13. Proverb about reputation and character

14. Regard as insignificant

15. Warning about undue modesty

AFRAID OF THE DARK

1. *The Dark Frigate*

2. *Journey in the Dark*

3. Dark Ages

4. Dark and Bloody Ground

5. Dark Continent

6. Dark horse

7. *The Dark Flower*

8. Dark lady of the sonnets

9. *Dark Laughter*

10. *The Dark Lady of the Sonnets*

11. A leap in the dark

12. The darkest hour is that before the dawn.

13. "Reputation is what you are in the Light; character is what you are in the Dark."

14. Make light of

15. Don't hide your light under a bushel.

THE MINUTIAE OF COME

We invite guests to "Come in." We depress pretentious claims with "Oh, come off it." All answers below confirm the versatility of a word we've used since our primers commanded, "Come, cat, come. Come, kittens, come."

1. Happen

2. To meet by chance

3. Slang for repeat

4. To cause separation or estrangement

5. To be eligible for

6. To recover consciousness

7. Why?

8. Slang, to do or give what is wanted

9. Scold

10. Inherit

11. Volunteer one's services, or give information

12. Happen

13. Formal social debut

14. To propose

15. Disclose publicly

THE MINUTIAE OF COME

1. Come about

2. Come across

3. Come again

4. Come between

5. Come in for

6. Come to

7. How come?

8. Come across

9. Come down upon

10. Come into

11. Come forward

12. Come off

13. Come out

14. Come up with

15. Come out with

AGED WORDS

"Old age," said Golda Meier, "is like a plane flying through a storm. Once you're aboard, there's nothing you can do." The answers to this quiz were equally powerless against the insidious onslaught of "age". Example: Pay — Wage.

1. Folk wisdom

2. Playful banter

3. Belittle

4. Scrounge

5. Hay

6. Statue

7. Conduct

8. Public institution for children

9. Carrying boats and supplies overland

10. Devastates

11. Guardianship

12. Custom

13. A position likely to provide superiority

14. Burg

15. Face

AGED WORDS

1. Adage

2. Badinage

3. Disparage

4. Forage

5. Herbage

6. Image

7. Manage

8. Orphanage

9. Portage

10. Ravage

11. Tutelage

12. Usage

13. Vantage

14. Village

15. Visage

THAT VERSATILE CEREAL!

From Spanish rice to rice pudding, from diet staple to wedding rite, from proper noun to part of the innards of a word, rice has been around the block. Now you'll be the sleuth who will discover rice in every answer below.

1. Bobolink

2. An impulsive change of mind

3. Houston university

4. A very short period of time

5. American playwright whose original surname was Reizenstein

6. Powder or paste for cleaning teeth

7. Author of *Mrs. Wiggs of the Cabbage Patch*

8. Cost

9. Well-known sportswriter

10. Greed

11. Female name

12. Gary Hart's *cherie amie*

13. Three times

14. Novel by Arnold Bennett about a parsimonious pair who starved themselves to death

15. Candy

THAT VERSATILE CEREAL!

1. Rice bird

2. Caprice

3. Rice

4. Trice

5. Elmer Rice

6. Dentifrice

7. Mrs. Alice Caldwell Rice nee Hegan

8. Price

9. Grantland Rice

10. Avarice

11. Beatrice

12. Donna Rice

13. Thrice

14 *Riceyman Steps*

15. Licorice

PLAIN TALK

All answers in this exercise contain "plain". It may be an adjective or a noun. Example: French-named Illinois city reflecting state's topography — Des Plaines.

1.   The site of Stonehenge

2.   Open view

3.   Battle site near Quebec

4.   Gregorian chant

5.   Member of a police force

6.   Easy progress

7.   Members of the Amish, Dunker and Mennonite sects

8.   Dakotas, Blackfeet, Cheyennes

9.   Poem by Bret Harte

10.   Comedy by William Wycherley

11.   Volume of short stories by Rudyard Kipling

12.   Patricia MacLachlan's Newbery Medal book about a stepmother

13.   Cleveland, Ohio, newspaper

14.   Obvious

15.   Brutally frank

PLAIN TALK

1. Salisbury Plain

2. Plain sight

3. Plains of Abraham

4. Plainsong

5. Plainclothes man

6. Plain sailing

7. Plain People

8. Plains Indians

9. *Plain Language from Truthful James*

10. *The Plain Dealer*

11. *Plain Tales from the Hills*

12. *Sarah Plain and Tall*

13. *Plain Dealer*

14. Plain as the nose on your face

15. Plain-spoken

WHAT'S IN A NAME

All the clues below will yield a given name. Example: Abraham Lincoln's only son to survive childhood. — Robert.

1. Feminine version of that borne by crown prince of Monaco

2. Her first fame came with a state fair blue ribbon for biscuits

3. Edgar Allan Poe mourned a lost love

4. The first actress to win an Oscar

5. A carriage favored by a duke before he became William IV of England

6. A town in northeast Missouri

7. Household word because of certain food offerings

8. A firework similar to a pinwheel

9. Wife of Menelaus, abducted by Paris to precipitate Trojan War

10. Feminine version of Aramaic word for lord

11. Author of *The Yearling*

12. Female Supreme Court Justice, not Sandra

13. Alamo victim who had popularized knife designed by his brother

14. Name shared by 1946 and 1958 Miss Americas

15. An Olympic star

WHAT'S IN A NAME

1. Alberta

2. Donna

3. Lenore

4. Janet

5. Clarence

6. Edina

7. Betty

8. Catherine

9. Helen

10. Martha

11. Marjorie

12. Ruth

13. James

14. Marilyn

15. Mary Lou

BACK A WINNER

With all its nuances. Example: A blow with the back of the hand.
— Backhander.

1. Poem by James Whitcomb Wiley

2. Forsake

3. Slander

4. Unknown workers in all branches of technology

5. Private or unrecognized power

6. Area in which one is isolated from active flow of life

7. In football, players behind line of scrimmage

8. Antagonistic reaction

9. Machine used in excavating

10. Poem by James A. Bland

11. Publisher's posting of older titles

12. Great Outback of Australia

13. Row backward

14. Wrestling term for completely beaten

15. Retreat from a difficult position

BACK A WINNER

1. *Back to Griggsby's Station*

2. Turn one's back on someone

3. Backbite

4. Backroom boys

5. Backstairs influence

6. Backwater

7. Backfield

8. Backlash

9. Backhoe

10. *Carry Me Back to Old Virginny*

11. Backlist

12. Back-of-Beyond

13. Back the oars

14. Thrown on his back

15. Back out

OPEN, SESAME

Remember the passwords that opened the robbers' cave in *Ali Baba and The Forty Thieves*? "Open" is the password for this exercise's answers. Example: Private opinion is allowed about a statement or fact — Open question.

1. Occurring or existing outdoors

2. Easily settled

3 Contest in which both professionals and amateurs participate

4. Speak unrestrainedly

5. Municipality that is declared demilitarized

6. Course set in 1899 for China

7. In chemistry, a linear arrangement of atoms

8. A mutual fund

9. First event in a series

10. Volume for which Louis Simpson won Poetry Pulitzer in 1964

11. Watchful and alert

12. Certain sandwiches

13. Generous

14. Medical procedure

15. Used in the production of high-quality steel

OPEN, SESAME

1. Open-air

2. Open-and-shut

3. Open

4. Open up

5. Open city

6. Open Door Policy

7. Open chain

8. Open-end investment company

9. Opener

10. *At The End of the Open Road*

11. Open-eyed

12. Open-faced

13. Open-handed

14. Open heart surgery

15. Open hearth

15 PIECES OF SILVER

Every answer contains "silver". Example: Novel by Phyllis A. Whitney — *Silverhill or The Quicksilver Pool.*

1. A paper money bill, formerly issued as legal tender

2. Wingless insect that damages book bindings, starched clothing, etc.

3. A color phase of the North American red fox

4. Used in photography, mirror manufacture, hair dye, etc.

5. A fish, the mademoiselle

6. Person who makes or repairs articles of silver

7. U.S. military decoration for gallantry in action

8. Eloquent

9. Prospect of better days

10. Born to good luck

11. Lone Ranger's horse

12. If a word be worth one shekel, silence is worth two.

13. A kidnapper

14. Name given in amused contempt to novelists who favored exaggerated etiquette

15. English Channel

15 PIECES OF SILVER

1.   Silver certificate

2.   Silverfish

3.   Silver fox

4.   Silver nitrate

5.   Silver perch

6.   Silversmith

7.   Silver Star

8.   Silver-tongued

9.   Every cloud has a silver lining.

10.   Born with a silver spoon in one's mouth

11.   Silver

12.   Speech is silver; silence is golden.

13.   The silver cooper

14.   The Silver Fork School

15.   The Silver Streak

ON THE ROAD

All answers include "road". Example: Highway intersecting with another — Crossroad.

1. Selfish and reckless driver

2. Foundation of a railroad

3. Question of futility

4. 1943 Newbery Medal book by Elizabeth Janet Gray

5. Become a vagabond

6. Barricade

7. Novel by Robert Nathan

8. Proverb about reaching the summit

9. Roger Miller song

10. Bandit who robbed stagecoaches

11. Inn, restaurant or nightclub located outside city

12. Proverb pertaining to illness

13. Comedy written by Robert Sherwood

14. Poem by Charles Divine

15. Swift-running, crested bird

ON THE ROAD

1.   Road hog

2.   Roadbed

3.   What is the use of running if one is not on the right road?

4.   *Adam of the Road*

5.   Take to the road.

6.   Roadblock

7.   *Road of Ages*

8.   "You must travel over a rough road to reach the stars."

9.   *King of the Road*

10.   Road agent

11.   Roadhouse

12.   "Illness arrives by many roads, but always is uninvited."

13.   *The Road to Rome*

14.   *We Met on Roads of Laughter*

15.   Roadrunner

SOME LIKE IT HOT

If the weather outside is frightful, warm yourself with the heat of this quiz. Every answer is a hot one.

1.   Empty talk

2.   Christmas game

3.   Sweet bread associated with Lent

4.   With speed

5.   Planning an unpleasant experience for someone

6.   Pungent fruit or condiment

7.   Alcoholic beverage

8.   Incredibly successful sale

9.   Not very satisfactory

10.   To be inconsistent

11.   To get into difficulties

12.   A fiery person

13.   Angry

14.   An overheated axle

15.   Frankfurter served in a long, soft roll

SOME LIKE IT HOT

1. Hot air

2. Hot cockles

3. Hot cross buns

4. Hot-foot

5. I'll make this place too hot to hold her/him.

6. Hot pepper

7. Hot toddy

8. Sold like hot cakes

9. Not so hot

10. Blow hot and cold

11. Get into hot water

12. Hothead or hotspur

13. Hot under the collar

14. Hot box

15. Hot dog

CALENDARS UNMARKED FOR THESE AFRICAN-AMERICAN ACHIEVERS

1.	Who led colonists that clashed with the British in the 1770 Boston Massacre?

2.	Who was the author of *Go Tell It on the Mountain*?

3.	Who was the first black American to publish a novel?

4.	What pioneer inventor obtained patents for a corn planter and cotton planter?

5.	Who, educated in Iowa, revolutionized the economy of the South?

6.	Who was the first black general in the U.S. Army?

7.	Who is called the father of Africa-American art?

8.	Who edited the abolitionist weekly *The North Star*?

9.	Who was the first American decorated by France in World War I?

10.	Who supervised installation of the first electric street lighting in New York City?

11.	Who was the first black justice of the U.S. Supreme Court?

12.	Who was a Navy hero of the Pearl Harbor attack?

13.	Who invented a vacuum pan evaporator, revolutionizing the sugar-refining industry?

14.	Who was the actor-singer who was graduated first in his class at Rutgers in 1913?

15.	Who was the first best-selling black American novelist?

CALENDARS UNMARKED FOR THESE AFRICAN-AMERICAN ACHIEVERS

1.   Crispus Attucks

2.   James Baldwin

3.   William Wells Brown

4.   Henry Blair

5.   George Washington Carver

6.   Benjamin O. Davis, Sr.

7.   Aaron Douglas

8.   Frederick Douglass

9.   Henry Johnson

10.   Lewis H. Latimer

11.   Thurgood Marshall

12.   Dorie Miller

13.   Norhert Rillieux

14.   Paul Robeson

15.   Frank Yerby

ON THE FACE OF IT

A little boy, visiting a pumpkin patch before Halloween, asked his father, "Where do they grow the ones with faces?" Lest you wonder, a "face" is in every answer to the following clues. Example: Oppose violently and unreasonably — Fly in the face of.

1.   In each other's presence

2.   Despite opposition

3.   To make an appearance

4.   Confronting one in the flesh

5.   To overcome by a stare or resolute manner

6.   To confront bravely

7.   To endure to the end

8.   To start play in hockey or other games

9.   King, queen or jack in a deck of playing cards

10.   Apparent value or significance

11.   Derogatory remark about a homely person

12.   Tale by Nathaniel Hawthorne

13.   Poem by H. Antoine D'Arcy

14.   The surface of a body of type that makes the impression

15.   Hypocritical

ON THE FACE OF IT

1. Face to face

2. In the face of

3. Show one's face

4. To one's face

5. Face down

6. Face up to

7. Face out

8. Face off

9. Face card

10. Face value

11. A face only a mother could love

12. *The Great Stone Face*

13. *The Face Upon The Floor*

14. Type face

15. Two-faced

GROUND WORK

Do you dig it? Every answer contains "ground". Example: A batted ball that hits the dirt before being caught by a fielder — Ground ball or grounder.

1.   To cut or dig into the earth.

2.   Travel over a considerable distance

3.   Leaving out nothing

4.   To make progress

5.   Maintain one's position

6.   Yield an advantage.

7.   Take another position

8.   In a familiar area

9.   To overdo to the point of being tedious

10.   Round, flesh fruit enclosed in a papery husk

11.   To work on a project from its inception

12.   Team of mechanics that service aircraft

13.   Woodchuck

14.   Unsubstantiated

15.   Low-growing plants that tend to prevent soil erosion

GROUND WORK

1. Break ground

2. Cover ground

3. From the ground up

4. Gain ground

5. Stand one's ground

6. Give ground

7. Shift one's ground

8. On home ground

9. Run into the ground

10. Ground cherry

11. Get in on the ground floor

12. Ground crew

13. Groundhog

14. Groundless

15. Ground cover

IT'S A BLOODY MESS!

1. What statement of Winston Churchill's was often quoted during World War II?

2. Anger, quarrel

3. Relationship has a claim

4. Money paid to a person for betraying another

5. It is inherited or exists in the family or race

6. Provokes indignation and anger

7. What was General George Patton's nickname?

8. Your children

9. Fresh members

10. Dogs used for tracking

11. Parasite

12. Frequent result of a playground fight

13. Variety of wheat

14. A book written by Truman Capote

15. Aristocrats

IT'S A BLOODY MESS!

1.   "I have nothing to offer but blood, toil, tears and sweat."

2.   Bad blood

3.   Blood is thicker than water.

4.   Blood money

5.   It runs in the blood.

6.   It makes one's blood boil.

7.   Old Blood-and-Guts

8.   Your own flesh and blood

9.   Young blood

10. Bloodhounds

11. Bloodsucker

12. Bloody nose

13. Bloody Mars

14. *In Cold Blood*

15. Bluebloods

HE'LL CUT UP WELL...

is a cynical remark about a rich man who will leave handsome portions to his heirs. A cut-up is a comic. He/she "cut up something fierce" may indicate a tantrum or a paroxysm of grief. All exercise answers use the three-letter verb "cut".

1.   There's plenty of it; have as much as you like.

2.   Already settled

3.   Be off as quickly as possible

4.   Sea superstition

5.   Be of no account

6.   Make an impression

7.   Entirely false

8.   Sailor's phrase for appearance of a face

9.   Disinherited

10.   Live within your means

11.   Reach years of discretion

12.   Cunning outwitting cunning

13.   Die prematurely

14.   Leave

15.   Make a show

HE'LL CUT UP WELL

1.   Cut and come again

2.   Cut and dried

3.   Cut and run

4.   Cut neither nails nor hair at sea.

5.   Cut no ice

6.   Cut a swath

7.   Cut out of whole cloth

8.   Cut of his jib

9.   Cut off with a shilling

10.   Cut your coat according to your cloth.

11.   Cut your wisdom teeth

12.   Diamond cut diamond

13.   One's life was cut short

14.   Cut one's stick

15.   Cut a dash

BEGINNING AND END

Each of the following clues has an answer in which the first letter is the same as the last letter. Example: loss of memory — Amnesia.

1.   Pertaining to the clergy

2.   A bird

3.   Boat

4.   A province in Canada

5.   Feudal estate

6.   Hawaiian greeting

7.   Form of address to a woman

8.   To roll about clumsily

9.   A gas used in lighted signs

10. Former name of Ethiopia

11. Payment to stockholders

12. Terrorist weapon

13. Exploit

14. Cupboard with drawers for storage

15. A place for performances

BEGINNING AND END

1.   Cleric

2.   Eagle

3.   Kayak

4.   Alberta or Ontario

5.   Fief

6.   *Aloha*

7.   Madam

8.   Wallow

9.   Neon

10.   Abyssinia

11.   Dividend

12.   Bomb

13.   Deed

14.   Hutch

15.   Arena

CLIMB EVERY MOUNTAIN

A mountain often looms in a book title. Occasionally, the mountain multiplies. All the listed authors climbed the heights at least once. Name the books. Example: Valerie Staats — *Between Mountain and Sea*.

1.   Bruce Brown

2.   Bianca Bradbury

3.   Dee Brown

4.   LeGrand Cannon, Jr.

5.   Gladys Hasty Carroll

6.   David Guterson

7.   Martha Ferguson McKeown

8.   Roger C. Palme

9.   Rosamunde Pilcher

10.   Emilie Irvin Powell

11.   Deane C. Davis

12.   Richard C. Davids

13.   Harnett T. Kane

14.   Robert Olen Butler

15.   Jan Karon

CLIMB EVERY MOUNTAIN

1. *Mountain in the Clouds*

2. *Andy's Mountain*

3. *Killdeer Mountain*

4. *Look to the Mountain*

5. *Man on the Mountain*

6. *East of the Mountains*

7. *Mountains Ahead*

8. *Living on the Mountain*

9. *Wild Mountain Thyme*

10. *Gracie and the Mountain*

11. *Justice in the Mountains*

12. *The Man Who Moved A Mountain*

13. *Miracle in the Mountains*

14. *A Good Scent from A Strange Mountain*

15. *In This Mountain*

MONEY IS EVERYTHING....

in this quiz. You are given a portion of a quotation about the green stuff, and you can put money on being in the money if you can complete the quotation. Example: Tell a miser he is rich, and a woman she is old; you'll get no money of one, no kindness of the other.

1.   Cleanliness is a priority, even...

2.   He who has money has a devil at his door; he who has...

3.   ...money is master.

4.   When it is a question of money, ...

5.   If you would lose a troublesome visitor, ...

6.   Would you know the value of money, ...

7.   A man without money is...

8.   Money is a good servant, ...

9.   Dally not with other men's...

10.   Never spend your money...

11.   Put not your trust in money, but...

12.   Money...

13.   Who marries for love without money has...

14.   An old man continues to be young in two things: ...

15.   In the hum of the market is money, but...

MONEY IS EVERYTHING

1.   ....if you don't have money for salt.

2.   ...no money has two devils.

3.   In all places...

4   ..., everybody is of the same opinion.

5.   ..., lend him money.

6.   ..., go and borrow some.

7.   ...a bow without an arrow.

8.   ..., but a dangerous master.

9.   ...women or money.

10.   ...before you have it.

11.   ...your money in Trust.

12.   ...isn't everything.

13.   ...good nights and sorry days.

14.   ...: love of money and love of life.

15.   ...under the cherry tree there is rest.

WHAT'S COOKIN'?

Terms associated with cuisine have been applied to human beings under various circumstances.

1. Someone very angry

2. To flatter

3. Get into trouble

4. Make a fatal mistake

5. Suddenly cease speech

6. The mouth

7. Good appetite

8. Unflappable

9. Stingy, ill-tempered person

10. Aristocrat

11. Anything unexpectedly easy

12. Yeoman of the English Guard

13. Attractive young female

14. Chubby child

15. Spend money

WHAT'S COOKIN'?

1.   Boiling or burning

2.   Butter up

3.   Get into hot water

4.   Cook one's goose

5.   Clam up

6.   Potato trap

7.   Fine knife and fork person

8.   Cool as a cucumber

9.   Crab

10.   Upper crust

11.   Piece of cake or easy as pie

12.   Beef-eater

13.   Tomato or chick

14.   Little dumpling

15.   Fork out

FLAME THROWERS

All answers relate to fire.

1.   Apparatus for giving signal

2.   Hydrant

3.   Meteor

4.   Hot-headed person

5.   One who inflames the passions of others

6.   Electrical luminosity on ships on dark, stormy nights

7.   An incendiary

8.   Combustible gas in coal mines

9.   Small explosive device

10.   Dalmatian

11.   Plan for quick exit of building

12.   Winged insect

13.   Shovel, poker and tongs

14.   Proverb

15.   Incombustible

FLAME THROWERS

1. Fire alarm

2. Fire plug

3. Fireball

4. Fire eater

5. Firebrand

6. St. Elmo's fire

7. Firebug

8. Fire damp

9. Firecracker

10. Fire department dog

11. Fire escape

12. Firefly

13. Fire irons

14. "If you will enjoy the fire, you must put up with the smoke."

15. Fireproof

SEA POWER...

surges into this exercise with a wave in every answer. Example:
Poem by Alan Cunningham — *A Sea Song.*

1.   Able to walk on deck when ship is rolling

2.   Cotton grown on coast of South Carolina

3.   Drogue

4.   Member of U.S. Navy construction battalion

5.   Hardtack

6.   Manatee or dugong

7.   Sailor with long experience

8.   Nellie Bly

9.   Aircraft

10.   Book authored by Laura Hillenbrand

11.   June event in Mystic, Connecticut

12.   Pacific stories by Jack London

13.   Poem by Elizabeth Akers Alien

14.   Novel by Jack London

15.   Book of poetry by Henry Wadsworth Longfellow

SEA POWER

1. Has sea legs

2. Sea Island cotton

3. Sea anchor

4. Seabee

5. Sea biscuit

6. Sea cow

7. Sea dog

8. Elizabeth Cochrane Seaman

9. Seaplane

10. *Seabiscuit*

11. Sea Music Festival

12. *South Sea Tales*

13. *Sea-Birds*

14. *The Sea-Wolf*

15. *The Seaside and The Fireside*

IT'S ALL COMING UP ROSES

1.   Matriarch of Massachusetts political family

2.   Site of presidential news conferences

3.   Indian reservation in South Dakota

4.   Japanese propagandist during World War II

5.   Younger sister of Queen Elizabeth II

6.   In strictest confidence

7.   Thirty years of war in England

8.   Shrub in the sandy Middle East

9.   An easy existence

10. Life so often has problems

11. Liquid used to improve women's complexions

12. Feature of Notre Dame cathedral

13. Shrub having lavender, yellow or white blossoms

14. Used as gemstone

15. Theatrical producer, author, songwriter, husband of Fanny Brice

IT'S ALL COMING UP ROSES

1. Rose Kennedy

2. White House Rose Garden

3. Rosebud

4. Tokyo Rose

5. Margaret Rose

6. Under the rose (*Sub rosa*)

7. Wars of the Roses

8. Rose of Jericho

9. Bed of roses

10. No rose without a thorn

11. Rosewater

12. Rose window

13. Rose of Sharon

14. Rose quartz

15. Billy Rose

BIRD IDENTIFICATION

All answers contain "bird". Example: Possession is better than expectation — A bird in the hand is worth two in the bush.

1. Shuttlecock used in badminton

2. Raven or owl

3. Silly, light-minded person

4. A temporary visitant

5. Claudia Alta Johnson

6. People who are alike in some way

7. Slang for a military officer

8. Experience teaches wisdom.

9. In golf, one stroke under par for any hole

10. The employee does the work; the employer makes the money.

11. Naval slang for aircraft carrier

12. Source of information

13. Cage star and coach

14. Sarcastic remark about overdressed person who does not live up to her/his clothes

15. To effect two objectives with outlay of one effort

BIRD IDENTIFICATION

1. Bird

2. Bird of ill-omen

3. Bird-brain

4. Bird of passage

5. Ladybird

6. Birds of a feather

7. Bird colonel

8. Old birds are not to be caught with chaff.

9. Birdie

10. One beats the bush; the other takes the bird.

11. Bird farm

12. A little bird told me.

13. Larry Bird

14. Fine feathers make fine birds.

15. To kill two birds with one stone

MEOW SWEET IT IS...

to salute America's favorite pet with a cat quiz. Example: Newbery Medal book by Elizabeth Coatsworth — *The Cat Who Went to Heaven.*

1.   An advantage of being a feline

2.   An inferior may have certain freedoms.

3.   A legend about a Lord Mayor of London

4.   Never

5.   Let a secret be known

6.   If a person is unwontedly silent

7.   Being too cautious can defeat one.

8.   A whistle or rude sound to express disapproval

9.   A deformity of fruit caused by insect sting or disease

10.   Ridiculous

11.   A gullywasher of a rain

12.   Very uneasy

13.   Lack of space

14.   Newbery Medal book by Emily Cheney Neville

15.   Series of titles by Lillian Jackson Braun

MEOW SWEET IT IS

1. A cat has nine lives.

2. A cat may look at a king.

3. Dick Whittington and his cat

4. Before a cat can lick her ear

5. Let the cat out of the bag

6. Cat got your tongue?

7. A cat in gloves catches no mice.

8. Catcall

9. Catface

10. Enough to make a cat laugh

11. It is raining cats and dogs.

12. Like a cat on hot bricks

13. No room to swing a cat

14. *It's Like This, Cat*

15. *The Cat Who...*

DOGGONE!

This exercise has gone to the dogs, a dog in every answer.
Example: Desist from some pursuit or inquiry — Call off the dogs.

1.   One who will not use what is wanted by another, nor yet
       let the other have it to use.

2.   The meanest thing with life in it is better than the noblest
       without it.

3.   You may crow over me today, but my turn will come by
       and by.

4.   Let well enough alone.

5.   Flower once believed to cure the bite of a mad dog

6.   Said of one who is sullen or sulky

7.   American identity discs, World War II

8.   Very sick

9.   Horrors of war — famine, sword, fire

10.   Guard duty aboard ship

11.   Have a shameful, or a miserable end

12.   Go to utter ruin

13.   Be bothered and harried from pillar to post

14.   A peninsula on the left bank of the Thames

15.   What Laplanders call the bear

DOGGONE!

1. A dog in the manger

2. A living dog is better than a dead lion.

3. Every dog has his day.

4. Let sleeping dogs lie.

5. Dog rose

6. No word to throw at a dog

7. Dog tags

8. Sick as a dog

9. Dogs of war

10. Dog watch

11. Die like a dog

12. Go to the dogs

13. Lead a dog's life

14. Isle of Dogs

15. Dog of God

HARE! HARE!

All answers refer to one of the long-eared, hopping brotherhood — be it bunny, hare or rabbit. Example: Appendage to television set — Rabbit ears.

1. John Updike's Pulitzer Prize winner in 1982

2. Updike's Pulitzer winner in 1991

3. Robert Lawson's Newberry Medal Book in 1945

4. British-born American war correspondent/photographer in Spanish-American War

5. English nobility

6. Children's favorite spring visitor

7. Aromatic shrub

8. *Tularemia*

9. A clover

10. A chopping blow to the back of the neck

11. A melted cheese dish served over toast

12. A dance in ragtime rhythm

13. Hugh Hefner's female charmers

14. Warner Brothers character

15. Order of 12 knights created by Edward III in France

HARE! HARE!

1. *Rabbit Is Rich*

2. *Rabbit at Rest*

3. *Rabbit Hill*

4. James H. Hare

5. Earls of Harewood

6. Easter rabbit

7. Rabbit brush

8. Rabbit fever

9. Rabbit foot

10. Rabbit punch

11. Welsh rabbit.

12. Bunny hug

13. Playboy Bunnies

14. Bugs Bunny

15. The Order of the Hare

TO HORSE!

Back in the Saddle Again, sang Gene Autry. Champion probably saw his share of tumblin' tumbleweeds — but no West Nile virus — before he came to the last round-up. Fifteen "horses" await your ropes, pardners. Example: Film about the U. S. West — horse opera.

1. A person whose capabilities may be unsuspected

2. A different affair altogether

3. Said of one who is determined not to take a hint

4. Very strong

5. When a present is offered, don't inquire into its value.

6. Trying to revive interest in an out-of-date subject

7. Don't be in such a hurry.

8. Direct from the highest authority

9. Everyone makes a mistake occasionally.

10. To make an error in judgment

11. To be overbearing and arrogant

12. To ride on Shank's mare

13. Reverses the right order

14. When obvious precautions are taken after a disaster

15. At some point, it is impossible to get an obstinate person to proceed.

TO HORSE!

1. Dark horse

2. A horse of another color

3. A nod is as good as a wink to a blind horse.

4. As strong as a horse

5. Don't look a gift horse in the mouth.

6. Flogging a dead horse

7. Hold your horses.

8. Straight from the horse's mouth

9. 'Tis a good horse that never stumbles.

10. To back the wrong horse

11. To be on one's high horse

12. To ride on the horse with ten toes (walk)

13. Set the cart before the horse

14. Lock the stable after the horse is stolen

15. You can lead a horse to water, but you can't make him drink.

IF A PIG FLIES

Often a response to wishful thinking. The conjunction begins every answer-proverb in this exercise.

1.   A jingle about ifs and wishful thinking

2.   They all look alike.

3.   Reaching out to others

4.   Keeping a secret

5.   Association with disreputable persons

6.   Owing

7.   Question about wealth

8.   No one can achieve the ends you desire as you can.

9.   Intimidation of aggressors

10.   Never let a barrier stop you.

11.   Advice for success

12.   Making do with what you have

13.   The right to be ostentatious

14.   Harry S. Truman's maxim

15.   Failure to have a spread for your bread

IF A PIG FLIES

1. If ifs and ans (sic)/Were pots and pans/Where would be the tinker?

2. If you've seen one, you've seen 'em all.

3. If you want friends, you must be one.

4. If you would keep your secret from an enemy, tell it not to a friend

5. If you lie down with dogs, you'll get up with fleas.

6. If you are in debt, somebody owns a part of you.

7. If your riches are yours, why don't you take them with you to the other world?

8. If you want something done right, do it yourself.

9. If you want peace, prepare for war.

10. If you can't jump over, crawl under.

11. If at first you don't succeed, try, try again.

12. If you have no bacon, you must be content with cabbage.

13. If you've got it, flaunt it.

14. "If you can't stand the heat, get out of the kitchen."

15. Ifs and Buts butter no bread.

ONE BY ONE

You'll find "one" in every answer. Example: Plea associated with Ronald Reagan — "One for the Gipper!"

1. Cyclops

2. A musical or dramatic performance

3. Biased

4. Ballroom dance

5. Former

6. Obsessively limited to single idea or purpose

7. Permitting movement in a single direction

8. A kind of pairing

9. Poem by Oliver Wendell Holmes

10. The Devil

11. Values are relative.

12. Part of the Pledge of Allegiance

13. Oneself

14. A costly victory

15. Everybody

ONE BY ONE

1.   Any of three one-eyed Titans

2.   One-night stand

3.   One-sided.

4.   One-step

5.   One-time

6.   One-track

7.   One-way

8.   One-to-one

9.   *The One-Hoss Shay*

10.   The Evil One

11.   One man's meat is another man's poison.
                          or
    One man's trash is another man's treasure.

12.   One nation under God

13.   Number One

14.   One more such victory, and we are lost.

15.   One and all

T IS FOR TWO

All answers contain the word "two". Example: An ageless idea —
There are two sure things — death and taxes.

1.　　To reach a correct conclusion

2.　　In baseball, a two-bagger

3.　　Worth very little

4.　　Twenty-five cents

5.　　A length of lumber

6.　　Sharp on both sides

7.　　Aggressive

8.　　Hypocritical

9.　　Golf club

10.　Deuce

11.　Unfaithful to loved one

12.　A ballroom dance

13.　Movie for which Sophia Loren won an Oscar in 1961

14.　Lyrics by Irving Caesar

15.　A Newbery Medal book by Sharon Creech

T IS FOR TWO

1. Put two and two together

2. Two-base-hit

3. Two-bit

4. Two bits

5. Two-by-four

6. Two-edged

7. Two-fisted

8. Two-faced

9. Two-iron

10. Two-spot

11. Two-time

12. Two-step

13. *Two Women*

14. *Tea for Two*

15. *Walk Two Moons*

ADDRESSING THREE

All answers contain the word. "three". Example: Movie entertainers — The Three Stooges.

1. Composition by Kurt Weill

2. Joanne Woodard won an Oscar for her role in this 1957 movie.

3. Sammy Cahn wrote the lyrics; Jule Styne, the music, for this song.

4. The site of a nuclear disaster

5. A proverb about friends for all occasions

6. A maxim about what wearies men

7. What members of the swine family were threatened by the big bad wolf?

8. What are a feeling in the heart, an expression in words and a giving in return?

9. Medical advice

10. Caution for heirs

11. Whence you came, where you are going and to whom you must account

12. Czech advice to a son

13. Money makes the world go around.

14. Who were Wynken, Blynken and Nod?

15. Poem by Henry Wadsworth Longfellow

ADDRESSING THREE

1. *Threepenny Opera*

2. *The Three Faces of Eve*

3. *Three Coins in the Fountain*

4. Three-Mile Island

5. "There are three faithful friends: an old wife, an old dog and ready money."

6. "After three days, men grow weary of a wench, a guest and rainy weather."

7. Three Little Pigs

8. Three forms of gratitude

9. Three good meals a day is bad living.

10. It is only three generations from shirt-sleeves to shirt-sleeves.

11. Think of these three things.

12. Before going to war, say one prayer; before going to sea, say two; before getting married, say three prayers.

13. He who economizes has as much as three others.

14. Three who went to fish for the herring-fish

15. *I Saw Three Ships*

THE VERSATILITY OF FOUR

All answers contain the word "four". Example: Forthright, frank —
Four-square.

1. Spring, summer, fall, winter

2. Book authored by Elisabeth Peters

3. An Alaska island.

4. Chief objectives of America and United Nations policy as
    proposed by Franklin D. Roosevelt

5. Inner circle of New York society

6. Conquest, Slaughter, Famine and Death

7. Set of Poems by Edmund Spenser

8. Opening of Gettysburg Address

9. The daily press

10. Independence Day

11. Fifty cents

12. Bluffer or faker

13. In poker, a five-card hand having four cards in same suit

14. Lake in Switzerland

15. Youth organization

THE VERSATILITY OF FOUR

1. Four seasons

2. *The Night of Four Hundred Rabbits*

3. Island of the Four Mountains

4. Four Freedoms

5. The Four Hundred

6. The Four Horsemen of the Apocalypse

7. *Four Hymns to Love and Beauty*

8. "Fourscore and seven years ago ..."

9. Fourth Estate

10. Fourth of July

11. Four bits

12. Four-flusher

13. Four flush

14. Lake of the Four Forest Cantons

15. Four-H club

JILL HAD HER JACK, AND...

you have 15 of them. Every answer in this exercise refers to someone named. Jack.

1. Jacqueline Onassis' father

2. Hero of Daniel Defoe novel

3. Stuffed figure at which English boys throw sticks during Lent

4. Novel by Theodore Hook

5. Author of *On the Road*

6. Irishman who sought redress of grievances

7. Breed of Dog

8. Notorious English highwayman

9. Journalist

10. Nursery tale

11. He had an invisible coat, a cap of wisdom, shoes of swiftness and a resistless sword.

12. Nursery rhyme

13. Academy Award winner

14. He could eat no fat.

15. Heavyweight champion 1919-1926

JILL HAD HER JACK, AND

1. Jack Bouvier

2. Colonel Jack

3. Jack-a-Lent

4. *Jack Brag*

5. Jack Kerouvac

6. Jack Cade

7. Jack Russell

8. Jack Sheppard

9. Jack Anderson

10. Jack and the Beanstalk

11. Jack the Giant Killer

12. Little Jack Horner

13. Jack Lemmon, Jack Albertson, Jack Nicholson, Jack Palance

14. Jack Sprat

15. Jack Dempsey

SINGING THE BLUES

1.   Noble or aristocratic descent

2.   Official publication of British government

3.   Fly

4.   Stock that sells at a high price

5.   Depression

6.   Murderer of wives

7.   Eurasian plant naturalized throughout North America

8.   Style of jazz

9.   Heavy denim trousers

10.   Kentucky's nickname

11.   Rules designed to enforce certain moral standards

12.   Editing tool

13.   Person or ship from Nova Scotia

14.   Minnesota municipality

15.   Highest award

SINGING THE BLUES

1. Bluebloods

2. Blue book

3. Blue bottle

4. Blue chip

5. Blue devils

6. Bluebeard

7. Blue grass

8. Blues

9. Blue jeans

10. Blue Grass State

11. Blue laws

12. Blue pencil

13. Blue Nose

14. Blue Earth

15. Blue ribbon

A BROWN STUDY

All answers in this exercise contain "brown". Example: Partially refined sweet — Brown sugar.

1.   Author of *Kildeer Mountain*

2.   Author of *Dolley*

3.   Early British flintlock

4.   Abolitionist

5.   Footwear

6.   Joe Louis

7.   Slang for "fed up" in World War II

8.   Root beer float

9.   *Ursus arctos*

10.   Baked apple pudding

11.   Lignite

12.   Junior Girl Scout

13.   Nazi militia

14.   Trademark for a box camera

15.   Once widely used as a building material

A BROWN STUDY

1. Dee Brown

2. Rita Mae Brown

3. Brown Bess

4. John Brown

5. Buster Brown shoes

6. Brown Bomber

7. Brown off

8. Brown cow

9. Brown bear

10. Brown Betty

11. Brown coal

12. Brownie

13. Brown Shirts

14. Brownie

15. Brownstone

GOLD RESERVES

All answers, from single word to proverb, contain "gold". Example: On the Gulf of Guinea in western Africa — Gold Coast.

1. Worthless substitute sold

2. Someone invariably fortunate

3. In World War II, idling or shirking

4. Do not be deceived by appearance.

5. Andalusia

6. North American beetle

7. Woman who solicits gifts from men

8. Untroubled and prosperous era of history

9. A 50th commemorative occasion

10. A variety of corn

11. Mammon.

12. Practice moderation in all things.

13. Theft by Jason

14. Strait, named by Sir Francis Drake, connecting San. Francisco Bay and Pacific

15. Wildflower blooming in late sunnier or fall

GOLD RESERVES

1. Gold brick

2. Everything he/she touches turns to gold.

3. Gold-bricking

4. All that glitters is not gold.

5. Gold Purse of Spain (most fertile portion)

6. Gold bug

7. Gold-digger

8. Golden Age

9. Golden anniversary

10. Golden Bantam

11. Golden calf

12. Keep the golden mean.

13. Golden Fleece

14. Golden Gate

15. Goldenrod

GREEN GROW THE LILACS AND...

This salute to St. Patrick requires some writin' o' the green.

1. Golf course

2. Conservatory

3. "If they do these things in the ...., what shall be done in the dry?"

4. Legendary content of moon

5. Irish patriotic and revolutionary song

6. Jealousy

7. Men of Vermont

8. Legal tender in United States

9. A variety of plum

10. Attribute of successful gardener

11. Novice

12. St. Patrick's Day

13. Waiting area beyond stage in theater

14. Building-free area surrounding city

15. Crack troops in Vietnam

GREEN GROW THE LILACS AND...

1. Green

2. Greenhouse

3. Green tree

4. Green cheese

5. *The Wearing of the Green*

6. Green-eyed monster

7. Green Mountain Boys

8. Greenbacks

9. Greengage

10. Green thumb

11. Greenhorn

12. Green Ribbon Day

13. Green room

14. Greenbelt

15. Green Berets

THE RED, RED ROSE AND...

St. Joseph is the Czechs' patron saint, and red, the color of liberty — and magic — is their favored hue. All answers are partially red. Example: Indian chief: Red Cloud.

1.   In thieves' cant, a gold watch

2.   Caught in the act of committing

3.   North American duck

4.   Something that distracts attention

5.   Memorably happy day

6.   White rural laboring class in South

7.   Prepare for important visitor(s)

8.   Heated

9.   Reddish, hornless cattle

10. River rising in Texas Panhandle

11. Body of water separating Arabian Peninsula and Africa

12. Marine food fish

13. Impedimental use of official forms

14. A blackbird

15. Sequoia

THE RED, RED ROSE AND...

1. Red kettle

2. Redhanded

3. Redhead

4. Red herring

5. Red letter day

6. Rednecks

7. Roll out the red carpet

8. Red hot

9. Red polls

10. Red river

11. Red Sea

12. Red salmon; red drum (channel bass)

13. Red tape

14. Red-winged

15. Redwood